Dear Parent:

Your child's love of reading starts here!

Every child learns to read in a different way and at his or her own speed. Some go back and forth between reading levels and read favorite books again and again. Others read through each level in order. You can help your young reader improve and become more confident by encouraging his or her own interests and abilities. From books your child reads with you to the first books he or she reads alone, there are I Can Read Books for every stage of reading:

SHARED READING
Basic language, word repetition, and whimsical illustrations, ideal for sharing with your emergent reader

BEGINNING READING
Short sentences, familiar words, and simple concepts for children eager to read on their own

READING WITH HELP
Engaging stories, longer sentences, and language play for developing readers

READING ALONE
Complex plots, challenging vocabulary, and high-interest topics for the independent reader

I Can Read Books have introduced children to the joy of reading since 1957. Featuring award-winning authors and illustrators and a fabulous cast of beloved characters, I Can Read Books set the standard for beginning readers.

A lifetime of discovery begins with the magical words "I Can Read!"

Visit www.icanread.com for information
on enriching your child's reading experience.

I Can Read® and I Can Read Book® are trademarks of HarperCollins Publishers.

Go! Go! Cory Carson: Cory's First Day of School
Go! Go! Cory Carson™ © 2020 VTech.
Netflix is a trademark of Netflix, Inc. and is used with permission.
All rights reserved. Printed in the United States of America.
No part of this book may be used or reproduced in any manner whatsoever without written permission except
in the case of brief quotations embodied in critical articles and reviews. For information address HarperCollins
Children's Books, a division of HarperCollins Publishers, 195 Broadway, New York, NY 10007.
www.icanread.com

ISBN 978-0-06-300223-4

20 21 22 23 24 LSCC 10 9 8 7 6 5 4 3 2 1 ❖. First Edition

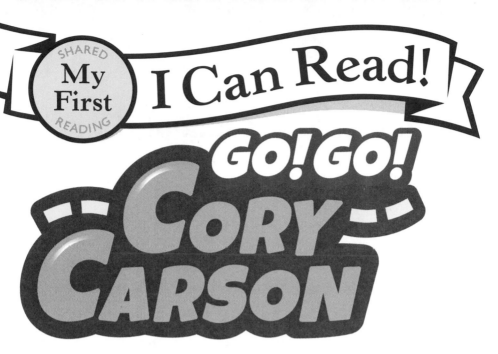

My First
SHARED
READING

I Can Read!

GO! GO! CORY CARSON

CORY'S FIRST DAY OF SCHOOL

Adapted by Megan Roth

Based on the episode
"Cory's First Day"
by Jason Heaton,
Stanley Moore, and
Alex Woo

HARPER
An Imprint of HarperCollinsPublishers

"It's time for school, Cory!"
Mom says.

"Almost forgot!" Cory says.

He gets out of bed fast.

"Where's my good morning hug?"
Mom asks.

Cory gives Mom a big hug.

"Let's get going!" he says.

First, Cory takes a bath.

Then, Cory eats breakfast.

Finally, it's time to go.

Mom and Cory drive over hills and through the town.

Cory is excited.

He made it to school!

"Welcome to Motorssori!"

Ms. Motors says.

She is Cory's new teacher.

Ms. Motors gives Cory
and Mom a tour.
There is a stage for music,
but the music is noisy.

There is a snack table,
but the snacks are strange.

Cory's first day is not
like he thought it would be.
"Mom, I want to go home,"
Cory says.

Mom goes to talk
to Ms. Motors.

Cory hasn't made
any friends yet.
He feels alone.

19

"Hey," a fire truck says.
"Can you help us?"

A group of friends
are building a block tower.
Cory brings them a block.

"Beautiful!" they cheer.

"Want to knock the tower over?" the crane asks.

Everyone laughs.

The friends knock it over together.

"Hi. I'm Freddie,"
the fire truck says.

"I'm Timmy," the loader says.
"I'm Kimmy!" the crane says.

"I'm Halle.
Want to play?"
the helicopter asks.

"Okay, Cory," Mom says.
"Let's go home."

But Cory has changed his mind.

"Can I stay?" he asks.

"Of course," Mom says.
"I'll see you after school."

"Hey, where's my goodbye hug?"
Cory asks.

Cory gives Mom a hug.
Have a great
first day, Cory!